ALPHABESTIARY

WORDSONG / BOYDS MILLS PRESS

ALPHA

ILLUSTRATED BY

Allan Eitzen

SELECTED BY

Jane Yolen

BESTIARY

To Kent, Clay, and Bee, who make it possible,
and to Joan O'Donnell, who makes it real—J.Y.

To grandsons Dietrich and Erich—A.E.

Published by Wordsong

Boyds Mills Press, Inc.

A Highlights Company

815 Church Street

Honesdale, Pennsylvania 18431

Printed in Mexico

Publisher Cataloging-in-Publication Data

Main entry under title.

   Alphabestiary : animal poems from a to z / selected by Jane Yolen ;
illustrated by Allan Eitzen.—1st ed.

[64]p. : col. ill. ;   cm.

Includes index.

Summary : A collection of poetry that celebrates animals from A to Z. Poems by William Blake,
Theodore Roethke, Isak Dinesen, and others are included.

ISBN 1-56397-222-0

1. Animals—Juvenile poetry. 2. Children's poetry. [1. Animals—Poetry.
2. Poetry—Collections.] I. Yolen, Jane. II. Eitzen, Allan, ill. III. Title.

808'.81—dc20   1995   CIP

Library of Congress Catalog Card Number 94-71021

First edition, 1995

Book designed by Joy Chu

The text of this book is set in 20-point Nicholas Cochin.

The illustrations are done in gouache, watercolor, and cut-paper collage.

Distributed by St. Martin's Press

10 9 8 7 6 5 4 3 2 1

Permission to reprint previously published material may be found on page 61.

CONTENTS

ANT SONG

The queen of ants she lays the eggs.
The males mate with the queen.
The workers find the food to eat
And keep the nest all clean.
The soldiers fight the enemy.
The nurses feed the young.
Ant on
Ant on
Ant on
Ant on
Ant now my song is sung.

– M a r y   A n n   H o b e r m a n

ANTEATER

I lie in wait
Without a plate,
My head upon my paws,
And soon the ants
Commence to dance
Into my toothless jaws.

Oh, what a life!
So little strife.
I scarce contain a yawn.
Just open wide—
They march inside,
And—with a snap—they're gone.

– J a n e   Y o l e n

THE BAT

By day the bat is cousin to the mouse.
He likes the attic of an ageing house.

His fingers make a hat about his head.
His pulse beat is so slow we think him dead.

He loops in crazy figures half the night
Among the trees that face the corner light.

But when he brushes up against a screen,
We are afraid of what our eyes have seen:

For something is amiss or out of place
When mice with wings can wear a human face.

—Theodore Roethke

CARVED BY ESKIMO WOMAN
STONE CUT, 24X37, 1961

Great Bear,
fur cut into stone.
Great Bear,
alone.
Sure of herself, slow,
what does the Great Bear,
bright bear,
straight from the heart of
night bear
know?

Great Bear knows
what the Eskimo knows.
Great Bear goes
where the Eskimo goes.
The woman who cut her into stone,
the woman who cut her, she alone
knows what the Great Bear,
night bear,
straight to the bright day
light bear
knows:

where she goes.

– Pat Schneider

THE COW

The friendly cow all red and white,
    I love with all my heart:
She gives me cream with all her might,
    To eat with apple-tart.

She wanders lowing here and there,
    And yet she cannot stray,
All in the pleasant open air,
    The pleasant light of day;

And blown by all the winds that pass
    And wet with all the showers,
She walks among the meadow grass
    And eats the meadow flowers.

— Robert Louis Stevenson

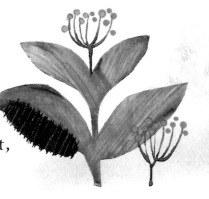

THE CATERPILLAR

Brown and furry
Caterpillar in a hurry
Take your walk
To the shady leaf or stalk
Or what not,
Which may be the chosen spot.
No toad spy you,
Hovering bird of prey pass by you;
Spin and die,
To live again a butterfly.

— Christina Rossetti

THE PRAYER OF THE CAT

Lord,
I am the cat.
It is not, exactly, that I have something to ask of You!
No—
I ask nothing of anyone—
but,
if You have by some chance, in some celestial barn,
a little white mouse
or a saucer of milk,
I know someone who would relish them.
Wouldn't You like someday
to put a curse on the whole race of dogs?
If so I should say,

Amen

—Carmen Bernos De Gasztold

TRANSLATED BY RUMER GODDEN

DONKEY

Donkey, donkey, old and grey,
Open your mouth and gently bray,
Lift your ears and blow your horn,
To wake the world this sleepy morn.

Donkey, donkey, do not bray,
But mend your pace and trot away;
Indeed, the market's almost done,
My butter's melting in the sun.

—Anonymous

WILD DUCKS

When ducks are crying
in the sky
and calling me
to rise and fly
I wish that I
were winged and wild,
a mallard
who was once a child.

—Sandra Liatsos

LONE DOG

I'm a lean dog, a keen dog, a wild dog, and lone;
I'm a rough dog, a tough dog, hunting on
   my own;
I'm a bad dog, a mad dog, teasing silly sheep;
I love to sit and bay the moon, to keep fat souls
   from sleep.

I'll never be a lap dog, licking dirty feet,
A sleek dog, a meek dog, cringing for my meat,
Not for me the fireside, the well-filled plate,
But shut door, and sharp stone, and cuff and kick
   and hate.

Not for me the other dogs, running by my side,
Some have run a short while, but none of them
   would bide.
O mine is still the lone trail, the hard trail, the
   best,
Wide wind, and wild stars, and hunger of the
   quest!

—Irene Rutherford McLeod

THE EAGLE

He clasps the crag with crooked hands;
Close to the sun in lonely lands,
Ringed with the azure world, he stands.

The wrinkled sea beneath him crawls;
He watches from his mountain walls,
And like a thunderbolt he falls.

— Alfred, Lord Tennyson

THE EMU

Let us emulate the emu
For the male sits on the nest
And he raises up the nestlings
With a fierce and joyous zest.
He is not emusculated
By his duties as a dad,
And the nestlings are elated
By the raising-up they've had.

— Jane Yolen

ELEPHANT

The elephant carries a great big trunk;
He never packs it with clothes;
It has no lock and it has no key,
But he takes it wherever he goes.

– Anonymous

FIREFLY

The firefly is a funny bug,
He hasn't any mind.
He blunders all the way through life
With his headlight on behind.

— Anonymous

THE FROG

Be kind and tender to the Frog,
    And do not call him names,
As "Slimy-skin," or "Polly-wog,"
    Or likewise "Ugly James,"
Or "Gap-a-grin," or "Toad-gone-wrong,"
    Or "Bill Bandy-knees":
The Frog is justly sensitive
    To epithets like these.
No animal will more repay
    A treatment kind and fair;
At least so lonely people say
Who keep a frog (and, by the way,
They are extremely rare).

— Hilaire Belloc

FISHES COME BITE!

Fishes come bite!
Fishes come bite!
I have fished all day;
I will fish all night.
I sit in the rain on my lily-leaf boat,
But never a minnow will bob my float.
Fishes come bite!

— Beatrix Potter

GRASSHOPPERS THREE

Grasshoppers three a-fiddling went,
Hey-ho, never be still!
They paid no money toward their rent
But all day long with elbow bent
They fiddled a tune called "Rill-a-be, rill-a-be"
Fiddled a tune called "Rill-a-be-rill."

— Old song

Ground Hog sleeps
All winter
Snug in his fur,
Dreams
Green dreams of
Grassy shoots,
Of nicely newly nibbly
Roots—
Ah, he starts to
Stir.

With drowsy
Stare
Looks from his burrow
Out on fields of
Snow.
What's there?
Oh no.
His shadow. Oh,
How sad!
Six more
Wintry
Weeks
To go.

— Lilian Moore

THE GAZELLE CALF

The gazelle calf, O my children,
goes behind its mother across the desert,
goes behind its mother on blithe bare foot
requiring no shoes, O my children!

– D . H . Lawrence

HORSES

Back and forth
and up and down
horses' tails go switching.

Up and down
and back and forth
horses' skins go twitching.

Horses do
a lot of work
to keep themselves from itching.

— Aileen Fisher

THE HAWK

Afternoon,
with just enough of a breeze
            for him to ride it
lazily, a hawk
sails still-winged
up the slope of a stubble-covered hill,
so low
he nearly
touches his shadow.

— Robert Sund

HAMSTERS

Hamsters are the nicest things
That anyone could own.
I like them even better than
Some dogs that I have known.

Their fur is soft, their faces nice.
They're small when they are grown.
And they sit inside your pocket
When you are all alone.

– Marci Ridlon

THE IRISH
WOLF-HOUND

As fly the shadows o'er the grass
   He flies with step as light and sure,
He hunts the wolf through Tostan pass
   And starts the deer by Lisanoure.
The music of the Sabbath bells,
   O Con! has not a sweeter sound
Than when along the valley swells
   The cry of John MacDonnell's hound.

His stature tall, his body long,
   His back like night, his breast like snow,
His foreleg pillar-like and strong,
   His hind leg like a bended bow,
Rough curling hair, head long and thin,
   His ear a leaf so small and round,—
Not Bran, the favorite dog of Fin,
   Could rival John MacDonnell's hound.

—Denis Florence McCarthy

IGUANA

Oh, iguana,
Do you wanna
Be a dragon
Or a snake?

With your scaley
Back and taily,
Do you hiss
Or do you bake?

Do you slither
Yon and hither,
Do you sail
Into the sky?

Oh, iguana,
Do you wanna
Eat a knight
Or eat a fly?

—Jane Yolen

JUNCO

The junco is a tiny bird,
But tougher than the rest,
Hopping up and crouching down
And puffing out its chest;
It flaps its wings and jumps about
When it comes time to feed.
I can't believe the fuss it makes
For one sunflower seed.

—Adam Stemple

JUMPING BEAN

A jumping bean
       is not a bean
I mean
Of course
       it is a bean
It's just that it's not just a bean
But something else as well (unseen).

A caterpillar
       (quite unseen)
Lives inside
       the jumping bean
And when the caterpillar bumps
Itself against the bean
       It jumps!*

*This caterpillar that I mean
(Which hides inside the jumping bean
And makes it hop upon the shelf)
Must be quite full of beans itself!

—Mary Ann Hoberman

THE KANGAROO'S COURTSHIP

"Oh will you be my wallaby?"
Asked Lady Kangaroo.
"For we could find so very many
Jumping things to do.
I have a pocket two feet wide
And deep inside,
My dear, you'd ride—
Oh, come, I'll be your bouncing bride,
Your valentine, your side-by-side,
I am in love with you."

—Jane Yolen

KOOKABURRA

Kookaburra sits on the old gum tree,
Merry, merry king of the bush is he.
Laugh, kookaburra, laugh, kookaburra,
Gay your life must be.

Kookaburra sits on the old gum tree,
Eating all the gum drops he can see.
Stop, kookaburra, stop, kookaburra,
Leave some there for me.

—Marion Sinclair

THE KAFFIR CAT

Alas for the kaffir cat
Once worshipped by the Pharoah,
Now Garfield, Morris, Felix and Bill
Are all the felines we know.

—Adam Stemple

THE LAMB

Little lamb, who made thee?
Dost thou know who made thee,
Gave thee life and made thee feed
By the stream and o'er the mead;
Gave thee clothing of delight,
Softest clothing, woolly, bright?
Gave thee such a tender voice,
Making all the vales rejoice?
Little lamb, who made thee?
Dost thou know who made thee?

Little lamb, I'll tell thee,
Little lamb, I'll tell thee!
He is called by thy name,
For He calls Himself a lamb.
He is meek, and He is mild;
He became a little child.
I a child, and thou a lamb,
We are called by His name.
Little lamb, God bless thee.
Little lamb, God bless thee.

— William Blake

LADYBIRD! LADYBIRD!

Ladybird! Ladybird! Fly away home,
Night is approaching, and sunset is come:
The herons are flown to their trees by the Hall;
Felt, but unseen, the damp dewdrops fall.
This is the close of a still summer day;
Ladybird! Ladybird! haste! fly away.

– Emily Brontë

LIZARD

A lizard ran out on a rock and looked up, listening
no doubt to the sounding of the spheres.
And what a dandy fellow! the right toss of a chin for you
And swirl of a tail!

If men were as much men as lizards are lizards
they'd be worth looking at.

– D.H. Lawrence

MULES

On mules we find two legs behind,
And two we find before.
We stand behind before we find
What the two behind be for.
When we're behind the two behind,
We find what these be for.
So—stand before the two behind,
Behind the two before.

– Old song

MONKEY, MONKEY

Monkey, monkey, sittin' on a rail,
Pickin' his teeth with the end of his tail.

— Anonymous

MICE

I think mice
Are rather nice.

Their tails are long,
Their faces small,
They haven't any
Chins at all.
Their ears are pink,
Their teeth are white,
They run about
The house at night.
They nibble things
They shouldn't touch
And no one seems
To like them much.

But I think mice
Are nice.

— Rose Fyleman

MOSQUITO

Onto a boy's arm came a mosquito.
"Don't hit! Don't hit!" it hummed.
"Grandchildren have I to sing to."
"Imagine," the boy said.
"So small and yet a grandfather."

— Eastern Eskimo

NIGHTHAWK

dives
  e
    a
      r
        t
          h
            w
              a
                r
                  d

tearing a hole
in soft,
    summer,
        dusk.

—Toni A. Watson

NEWT

Newt,
Eft,
Eft,
Newt,
A salamander
In a lizard suit.

—Jane Yolen

NIGHTJAR

Once I thought a nightjar
Was something by your bed
To hold your dreams and visions
Once they had left your head;
A crockpot full of images
You open with a word,
Till I found out the other day
It's just a silly bird.

—Adam Stemple

THE OCTOPUS

Tell me, O Octopus, I begs,
Is those things arms, or is they legs?
I marvel at thee, Octopus;
If I were thou, I'd call me Us.

—Ogden Nash

THE OSTRICH

The ostrich believes she is hidden from view
with her foolish head stuck in the ground.
For she thinks you can't see her when she can't see you,
so the ostrich is easily found.

—Jack Prelutsky

THE OWL

When cats run home and light is come,
　　And dew is cold upon the ground,
And the far-off stream is dumb,
　　And the whirring sail goes round,
　　And the whirring sail goes round;
　　　Alone and warming his five wits,
　　　The white owl in the belfry sits.

When merry milkmaids click the latch,
　　And rarely smells the new-mown hay,
And the cock hath sung beneath the thatch
　　Twice or thrice his roundelay,
　　Twice or thrice his roundelay;
　　　Alone and warming his five wits,
　　　The white owl in the belfry sits.

— Alfred, Lord Tennyson

THIS LITTLE PIGGY

This little piggy went to market,
This little piggy stayed home,

This little piggy had roast beef,
This little piggy had none,

And this little piggy cried, wee, wee, wee,
All the way home.

– Anonymous

THE PANTHER

The panther is like a leopard,
Except it hasn't been peppered.
Should you behold a panther crouch,
Prepare to say Ouch.
Better yet, if called by a panther,
Don't anther.

– Ogden Nash

THE PEACOCK

The over-ornate can be a burden as peacock
proves the weight of whose preposterous plumes
is psychological see how his peacock back is bent
hysterical he stamps his foot one more pavane
and I will scream he screams spreading once more
for the ten thousandth time that fantastic fan.

— Robert Francis

QUETZAL — QUIET!

Quetzal is the bird
of freedom, hiding
up in the canopy
of mist on the mountain.
Caged, Quetzal would die.

The Grandfathers'
green feathers made
the crowns of Maya
Indians,
Lords of the Mountains,
and their law said,

Quetzal may
not be killed.
Let shame chase any
who hurt these nests.
Leave them standing,

old, hollow trees
where Quetzal's sudden
call drops,
where Quetzal hops
off the perch backward

so that splendid
green
rain-
bow
of a
tail
won't
drag.

—Anna
Kirwan-Vogel

QUAIL

I took a walk
with a quail,
who followed me
and scratched his way
through leaves and dust,
thrusting his head forward,
a great soft chicken
of the forest.

– Ann Turner

THE TWO-HORNED
BLACK RHINOCEROS

The two-horned black rhinoceros
has nothing much to say,
and he tends to be unfriendly and unkind.

He's lumpy and he's grumpy
in a thick-skinned sort of way,
and there's nothing but a grumble on his mind.

—Jack Prelutsky

ROOSTER

If a rooster crows when he goes to bed
He'll get up with rain on his head.

– A n o n y m o u s

MISTER RABBIT

Mister Rabbit, Mister Rabbit,
Your ears are mighty long.
Yes, bless God, they were put on wrong.
Every little soul gonna shine, shine,
Every little soul gonna shine along.

Mister Rabbit, Mister Rabbit,
Your tail's mighty white.
Yes, bless God, I'm a gettin' out of sight.
Every little soul gonna shine, shine,
Every little soul gonna shine along.

Mister Rabbit, Mister Rabbit,
Your coat's mighty thin.
Yes, bless God, I'm a-cuttin' through the wind.
Every little soul gonna shine, shine,
Every little soul gonna shine along.

– O l d   s o n g

ABOUT THE TEETH
OF SHARKS

The thing about a shark is—teeth,
One row above, one row beneath.

Now take a close look. Do you find
It has another row behind?

Still closer—here, I'll hold your hat:
Has it a third row behind that?

Now look in and . . . Look out! Oh my,
I'll *never* know now! Well, goodbye.

—John Ciardi

SNAKE

I saw a young snake glide
Out of the mottled shade
And hang, limp on a stone:
A thin mouth, and a tongue
Stayed, in the still air.

It turned; it drew away;
Its shadow bent in half;
It quickened, and was gone.

I felt my slow blood warm.
I longed to be that thing,
The pure, sensuous form.

And I may be, some time.

—Theodore Roethke

THE SLOTH

In moving slow he has no Peer.
You ask him something in his ear,
He thinks about it for a Year;

And, then, before he says a Word
There, upside down (unlike a Bird),
He will assume that you have Heard—

A most Ex-as-per-at-ing Lug.
But should you call his manner Smug,
He'll sigh and give his Branch a Hug;

Then off again to Sleep he goes,
Still swaying gently by his Toes,
And you just *know* he knows he knows.

—Theodore Roethke

DELICATE
THE TOAD

Delicate the toad
Sits and sips
The evening air.

He is satisfied
With dust, with
Color of dust.

A hopping shadow
Now, and now
A shadow still.

Laugh, you birds
At one so
Far from flying

But have you
Caught, among small
Stars, his flute?

—Robert Francis

THE TIGER

Tiger! Tiger! burning bright
In the forests of the night,
What immortal hand or eye
Could frame thy fearful symmetry?

—William Blake from
"The Tiger"

TIGER

There was a young lady of Niger
Who smiled as she rode on a tiger.
　　They returned from the ride
　　With the lady inside—
And the smile on the face of the tiger.

—Anonymous

THE UMBRELLA BIRD

If I were to make a selection
Of evolution's strangest direction
With the weirdest of natural protection—
The umbrella bird would top my collection.

—Adam Stemple

UNICORN

The Unicorn with the long white horn
        Is beautiful and wild.
He gallops across the forest green
So quickly that he's seldom seen
Where Peacocks their blue feathers preen
        And strawberries grow wild.
He flees the hunter and the hounds,
Upon black earth his white hoof pounds,
Over cold mountain streams he bounds
        And comes to a meadow mild;
There, when he kneels to take his nap,
He lays his head in a lady's lap
        As gently as a child.

—William Jay Smith

THE UNICORN LEAVES

Deep, deep, deep in the cool
Forest, by a mirror pool
Lives the silken swift,
Lives the marble gift,
With a spiral horn.

Someday you may see him pass
As a shadow; hear the grass
Bend his steps. And hush!
Watch the poolside rushes
Parted by the horn.

The water bursts as if a gale
Started from his golden nail,
Bids them part. Then the sounds
Of horse and hounds,
And in a moment, he is gone.

—Jane Yolen

THE VULTURE

The Vulture eats between his meals,
  And that's the reason why
He very, very rarely feels
  As well as you and I.

His eye is dull, his head is bald,
  His neck is growing thinner.
Oh! what a lesson for us all
  To only eat at dinner!

– Hilaire Belloc

VOLE

Not half so famous as a mouse,
The tiny vole sits in her house.
Though she eats day and night, she gets no fatter,
Only angrier in her chatter.
For the owl, a tiny, angry bite
That's just right!

– Christine Crow

A WARBLER

In the sedge a tiny song
Wells and trills the whole day long;
In my heart another bird
Has its music heard.

As I watch and listen here,
Each to each pipes low and clear;
But when one has ceased to sing,
Mine will still be echoing.

—Walter de la Mare

WASPS

Wasps like coffee.
Syrup.
Tea.
Coca-Cola.
Butter.
Me.

—Dorothy Aldis

WOODPECKER IN DISGUISE

Woodpecker taps at the apple tree.
"Little bug, open your door," says he.
Little bug says, "Who is it, sir?"
Woodpecker says, "The carpenter."

– Grace Taber Hallock

THE WATERBEETLE

The waterbeetle here shall teach
A sermon far beyond your reach:
He flabbergasts the Human Race
By gliding on the water's face
With ease, celerity, and grace;
But if he ever stopped to think
Of how he did it, he would sink.

– Hilaire Belloc

XYLEBORUS

I would tell you if I could
Why xyleborus bores in wood.
It bores its way right through a tree,
Through bark and trunk so steadily
And just as surely it bores me!

—Jane Yolen

XIPHIAS GLADIUS

It carries a sword on the end of its nose,
Gets eXtremely eXcited in warm Southern seas
And rushes about like a Roman gladiator.
No wonder its name begins with an X,
The unknown quantity in algebra.
Its most eXpress wish
Is to slash into a school of smaller fish
And start to devour an unspecified number.
A fish of eXtraordinary ruthless X caliber!

– Christine Crow

THE YAK

As a friend to the children
   commend me the Yak.
     You will find it exactly the thing:
It will carry and fetch,
   you can ride on its back,
Or lead it about
   with a string.
The Tartar who dwells on the plains of Thibet
   (A desolate region of snow)
Has for centuries made it a nursery pet,
   And surely the Tartar should know!
Then tell your papa where the Yak can be got,
   And if he is awfully rich
He will buy you the creature—
   or else
         he will *not*.
(I cannot be positive which.)

—Hilaire Belloc

ZEMMI

In a deep, wet zone beneath the lime,
Even as you read this zany rhyme,
Zemmi the mole rat is giving birth
To a family of mole rats blind as herself.
      Half rat, half dog, half worm, half mole,
      That's far more halves than make a whole.

—Christine Crow

ZEBU

A cow—but not a cow—
and how:
a great big bump,
a shoulder hump;
a swallow flap
we call dewlap;
though milk and meat
are sweet
to eat
it's not a cow.
And how.

—Jane Yolen

ZEBRA

The eagle's shadow runs across the plain,
Towards the distant, nameless, air-blue mountains.
But the shadows of the round young Zebra
Sit close between their delicate hoofs all day, where
    they stand immovable,
And wait for the evening, wait to stretch out, blue,
Upon a plain, painted brick-red by the sunset,
And to wander to the water-hole.

—Isak Dinesen

ACKNOWLEDGMENTS

Every possible effort has been made to trace the ownership of each poem included in *Alphabestiary*. If any errors or omissions have occurred, corrections will be made in subsequent printings, provided the publisher is notified of their existence.

Permission to reprint poems is gratefully acknowledged to the following:

The Ciardi family for "About the Teeth of Sharks" by John Ciardi.

Christine Crow for "Vole," "Xiphias Gladius," and "Zemmi" by Christine Crow. Copyright © 1995 by Christine Crow.

Curtis Brown for "Quail" by Ann Turner. Copyright © 1995; and "Quetzal–Quiet!" by Anna Kirwan-Vogel. Copyright © 1995; and for "Junco," "Nightjar," "The Kaffir Cat," and "The Umbrella Bird" by Adam Stemple. Copyright © 1995 by Adam Stemple; and for "The Kangaroo's Courtship" by Jane Yolen. Copyright © 1987 and 1995 by Jane Yolen; and "The Unicorn Leaves," from *Here There Be Unicorns* by Jane Yolen. Copyright © 1994 by Jane Yolen; and "Anteater," "Iguana," "Newt," "The Emu," "Xyleborus," and "Zebu" by Jane Yolen. Copyright © 1995 by Jane Yolen. Reprinted by permission of Curtis Brown, Ltd.

Doubleday for "The Bat," copyright © 1938 by Theodore Roethke; "The Sloth," copyright © 1950 by Theodore Roethke; "Snake," copyright © 1955 by Theodore Roethke, from *The Collected Poems of Theodore Roethke* by Theodore Roethke; and for "Mice" from *Fifty-one New Nursery Rhymes* by Rose Fyleman. Copyright © 1931, 1932 by Doubleday, a division of Bantam Doubleday Dell Publishing Group, Inc. Used by permission of Doubleday, a division of Bantam Doubleday Dell Publishing Group, Inc.

Dutton Children's Books for "Woodpecker in Disguise" from *Bird in the Bush* by Grace Taber Hallock. Copyright © 1930 by E.P. Dutton, renewed © 1958 by Miss Grace Taber Hallock. Used by permission of Dutton Children's Books, a division of Penguin Books USA Inc.

Farrar, Straus & Giroux, Inc., for "Unicorn" from *Laughing Time: Collected Nonsense* by William Jay Smith. Copyright © 1990 by William Jay Smith. Reprinted by permission of Farrar, Straus & Giroux, Inc.

Florence Feiler for "Zebra" from *Out of Africa* by Isak Dinesen. Copyright © 1937, 1938 by Random House, Inc. Copyright renewed © 1965 by Rungstedlund Foundation. Reprinted by permission of Florence Feiler.

Greenwillow Books, a division of William Morrow & Company, Inc., for "The Ostrich" and "The Two-Horned Black Rhinoceros" from *Zoo Doings* by Jack Prelutsky. Copyright © 1967, 1974, 1983 by Jack Prelutsky.

HarperCollins for "Horses" from *Always Wondering* by Aileen Fisher. Copyright © 1991 by Aileen Fisher. Reprinted by permission of HarperCollins Publishers.

James Houston for "Mosquito" from *Songs of the Dream People: Chants and Images from the Indians and Eskimos of North America*, edited and illustrated by James Houston, Atheneum, New York. Copyright © 1972 by James Houston.

Little, Brown, and Company for "The Octopus" and "The Panther" from *Verses from 1929 On* by Ogden Nash. Copyright © 1940, 1942 by Ogden Nash. *First appeared in *The New Yorker*. By permission of Little, Brown and Company.

Gina Maccoby Literary Agency for "Ant Song" and "Jumping Bean" by Mary Ann Hoberman from *Bugs*. Copyright © 1976 by Mary Ann Hoberman. Reprinted by permission of Gina Maccoby Literary Agency.

Marci Ridlon McGill for "Hamsters" from *That Was Summer* by Marci Ridlon, Follett Publishing Company. Copyright © 1969 by Marci Ridlon.

Peters Fraser & Dunlop Group Ltd. for "The Frog," "The Vulture," "The Yak," and "The Waterbeetle" from *Complete Verse* by Hilaire Belloc, published by Pimlico, a division of Random Century. Reprinted by permission of the Peters Fraser & Dunlop Group Ltd.

G. P. Putnam's Sons for "Wasps" by Dorothy Aldis, reprinted by permission of G. P. Putnam's Sons from *Is Anybody Hungry?* by Dorothy Aldis, copyright © 1964 by Dorothy Aldis, copyright renewed © 1992 by Roy E. Porter.

INDEX

by *Title*, POET, and First Line